Biggles Adven...

A true story
about a young girls pet hamster

Round and round, round and round!!!

Biggles ran as fast as he could in his small wheel. He stopped and thought. I run as fast as I can but I never seem to get anywhere.

He decided to look for some sunflower seeds.
His tiny nose sniffed around, not a sunflower
seed to be seen. He could hear his owner singing
to herself as she tidied her bedroom.
Although there were other hamsters in several
cages around the room,

Biggles knew he was her favourite.
She would always take him out and cuddle him
the most. She even took him with her when she
went in the car with her mother.

She shared her food with him and talked to him, the thing he loved the most was chocolate.

It was probably quite bad for him but he still loved it.

Anyway, he still hadn't found any sunflower seeds and he was bored running around in his wheel. He looked out of the cage to see if he could see his owner, she had finished tidying and was fast asleep on her bed.

Fine, he thought, no sunflower seeds until morning. He wandered around the cage; he must have at least one sunflower seed hidden somewhere. You know how it is, the more you want something you haven't got,
the more you want it!

He climbed on top of his wheel but it turned around and slid him down to the bottom again. OK he thought to himself,
I'll try again.

This time just as the wheel slid around, he caught hold of the bars at the top of the cage, and hung there for a moment his back legs kicking in the air.

He managed to lift them up so he was clinging with all four feet. So, he thought to himself, fine! now what? I've got myself here what do I do now?

He began to edge his way along the bars, suddenly one of the bars moved, he took his paw away and tried again,

Yes it definitely moved. It was the cage door and it wasn't closed properly. This was his chance for freedom and to find a sunflower seed.

He edged nearer and pushed up with his nose, the door opened and he clambered out, this was interesting.

He ran along the shelf and lowered himself down to the next one, he did this again and again until he had managed to reach the floor. He looked up and could see the edge of his cage above him - his adventure had begun.

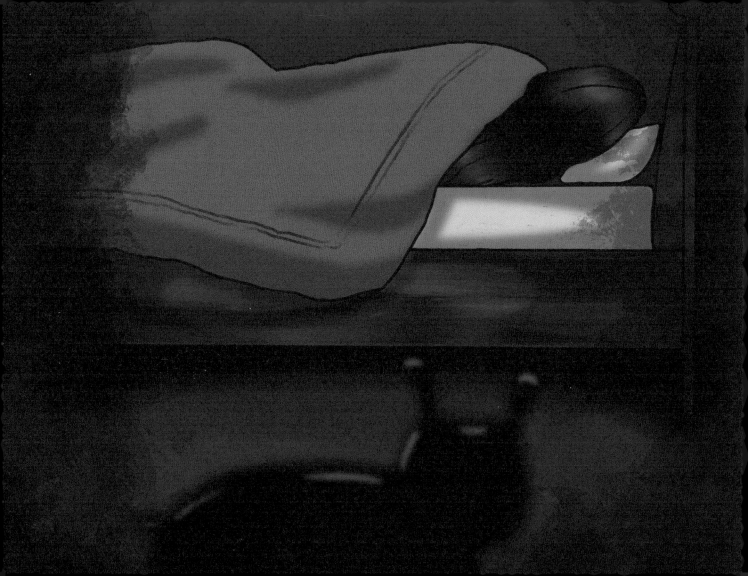

He could see his owner lying on the bed she gave a little sigh and turned over.

Biggles froze like a statue.

He wanted to go and say goodbye, he loved her dearly but he wanted an adventure and he knew she would give him a cuddle but put him back in his cage, and he had only just got out.

He stayed close to the edge of the bedroom wall, he ran past the bed and past the wardrobe, past his owner's school bag and shoes.

Suddenly he bumped into something large and furry, he turned and ran back then stopped. Very slowly he crept back and peeped around the chair.

There was another one next to it and this one was all brown. Biggles carefully walked past the black monster and looked up at a whole mountain of strange furry things.

They had fur but they were not like him. They were all different shapes and sizes and colours. beyond the pile of monsters was the door.

Biggles thought it's now or never, if they all pounce on me and eat me, fine! well not fine really

He reached the door, not one of them had moved, they just sat there all piled on top of one another, they must all be asleep he thought as he ran out the door.

Biggles didn't like open spaces so he crept along, close to the wall. If this is the outside world I'm not impressed, he said to himself.

He was wondering if he should go back to his cage when he noticed another open door. He ran into this room and stopped.

He didn't like the smells in this room. There were sweet smells, but there were very strong smells that nearly took his breath away.

It wasn't a very large room and there wasn't much in it. He followed the wall around and noticed a tiny opening. The door to freedom he thought, his adventure was getting better.

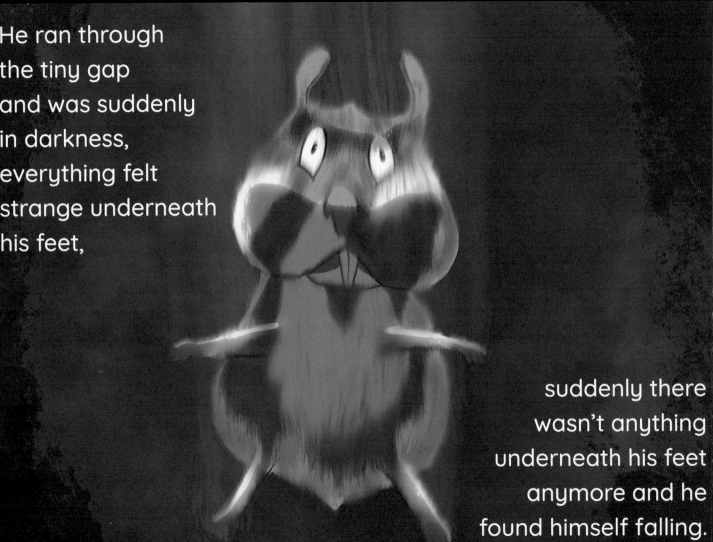

He ran through the tiny gap and was suddenly in darkness, everything felt strange underneath his feet,

suddenly there wasn't anything underneath his feet anymore and he found himself falling.

The fall knocked the wind out of him and he lay very still for a moment. He blinked his eyes and began to sneeze. He was covered in dust. He looked up and high above him was the hole he had fallen through.

He looked around, there was no way back up there. He was stuck, fine! he said to himself at least I'm free.

He became aware of the fact that he was feeling very hungry. I wonder if there are any sunflower seeds down here, he thought. He stood up and winced slightly.

He had hurt his back leg in the fall, he turned to look at it, nothing was broken so he decided to move on.

He hadn't gone very far when he walked into
something very sticky, like a sticky net?
it covered his face and was very unpleasant.

He stopped, sat on his hind legs and began
to wash his face with his front paws.

Something made his stop and look up.
Dangling in front of his face was a large spider
with black hairy legs.

He knew it was a spider because his owner did not like them and always ran out of the room screaming if she saw one.

Seeing one of them close up he understood why and he screamed a hamster scream and turned and ran too.

Biggles sat still for a little while and tried to clean his ears as they felt quite dusty, he wanted his ears to be clean so he could hear if his mistress was calling him.

Biggles knew he was lost, he didn't know whether to go left or right, try to climb up or down. He had no idea where he was, he was dirty, tired and very hungry and he needed a cuddle.

He seemed to be moving downwards and the more he moved the more difficult it was to go back.

He sat still for a moment and quietly cried to himself. He wished he had never started this adventure.

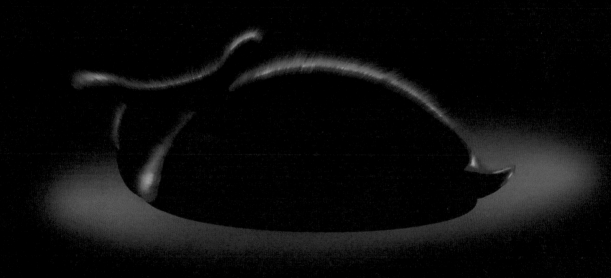

He wished he was curled up nice and warm in his little house in his very own cage with a secret stash of sunflowers. He finally fell asleep.

He was brought out of his thoughts by the sound of his owner's voice, in the distance, she sounded upset. He could hear her calling his name,

Biggles! Biggles! Biggles! Biggles!

"I'm here, he said, "please come and get me out of this horrible dark and dusty place - and there's a huge spider"! he thought about that last bit and said "well it's not that big really, it's quite small" he didn't want to scare her.

He could hear another voice say that they thought he had fallen down the hole under the bath and that he was probably inside the wall.

Fine! he thought so just break the wall and get me out. He waited and nothing seemed to happen, he could hear tapping on the wall, one almost next to him but now further down from him. He could also hear his owner still calling his name so he decided to move further downwards a little more.

He waited and waited and no-one came.

He only had a little sleep and suddenly woke up - what was that. He sniffed into the air, oh my, I can smell chocolate.

He began to follow the smell; it was definitely getting stronger and he could hear his owner calling his name again.

He stumbled on and soon he saw a light below him.

The smell of chocolate was very strong now and he thought he could even see a small, delicious, brown chunk waiting for him in the light.

I hope I'm not dreaming.

It was no dream as he reached the light and the chocolate, two loving hands reached in to grab him.

"Don't forget the chocolate" he said as his owner squeezed him tight and smothered him with kisses.

It was a good job there was a hole in the wall at the back of the electricity cupboard!

Later that night, after a warm bath,
Biggles lay in his little house.

What was left of the chocolate was hidden
in the corner for later with his sunflower seeds.

His adventure was over.

Printed in Great Britain
by Amazon

24231001R00021